ALEX RODRIGUEZ

Out of the Ballpark

illustrated by

Frank Morrison

AROD™

HarperCollinsPublishers

For the greatest gift God has given me,
my precious little angel, Natasha Alexander
—A.R.

I dedicate this to my home team:
my sons, Nyree, Tyreek, and Nasir; my daughter, Nia;
and my team's captain and my wife, Connie
—F.M.

BASEBALL.

Alex lived for it.

And it didn't get much better than this. His mom, brother, and sister were together in the stands for the first time all season. Today was the playoffs. Alex wanted to make them proud. He really wanted to win his first championship.

Crack!

The batter hit a ground ball toward second base.

Here it comes, Alex told himself. This will be an easy out.

He crouched to field the ball, just like he'd done a thousand times before . . .

. . . and the ball bounced between his legs.

   By the time the center fielder scooped it up,
the runner was safe at second.

   Alex looked up at his family in the stands.
His best friend, J.D., patted him on the back.

   "Relax," said J.D.

Alex tried to calm down. But the harder he tried, the worse he played.

"I think I'm setting a record for errors and strikeouts in the same game," he told J.D. in the last inning. "Good thing we're ahead—we have to win this game!"

"C'mon, Caribes!" Alex shouted to the team. "One more out!"

Pop! The batter's fly ball sailed into J.D.'s glove.

"**Yeeeaaaahhhhh**, J.D.!" Alex yelled. "We're going to the championship!"

But later that day, Alex couldn't help thinking about all the mistakes he'd made.

"Hey, Joe, will you throw me some pitches?" Alex asked his brother.

"Sure, slugger," Joe said.

Joe's first pitches were high, but Alex swung at all of them anyway.

"Settle down!" Joe said. "Wait for a pitch you can hit."

Alex knew Joe was right. He dug in and waited.
When a good pitch came, he swung smoothly.
Crack!
"Whoa," Joe said as he watched the ball soar.
"That would've been a pool shot!"

Alex laughed. Earlier in the season, he had hit a
home run into the swimming pool beyond the
Caribes' ballpark.

"Throw me another," Alex said.

The next morning, Alex got out of bed before the sun came up.
His clock read 5:02, but his body was ready to play ball.

He dialed J.D.'s number.

"Wake up!" Alex said. "Let's go hit
a few balls before school!"

"Are you crazy?" J.D. croaked.

But Alex was already out the door.

Alex and J.D. hit each other
fly balls.
And line drives.
And grounders.

With every ball Alex fielded, he pictured himself playing a
perfect championship game. His body tingled with excitement.

When the school bell rang, they raced inside. Their teacher, Ms. Gonzales, held her nose when they ran by.

"If we stink now, wait till after practice this afternoon," Alex whispered to J.D.

All week long, Alex and the other Caribes practiced their hearts
out. They ran faster, hit farther, and threw harder than ever before.

Alex took extra batting practice and tried to be patient at the plate,
but it was so tough. Every time he swung at an impossible pitch, he
remembered the playoff game. He felt a little sick inside.

What if I can't pull it together for the championship? he worried.

That night, Alex finished his homework and thought about the big game.

He threw a rubber ball against the wall, then caught it.

Thump-catch-thump-catch-thump-catch . . .

Five hundred times, Alex threw the ball against the wall.

Five hundred times, he caught it.

And every time he missed, he started over.

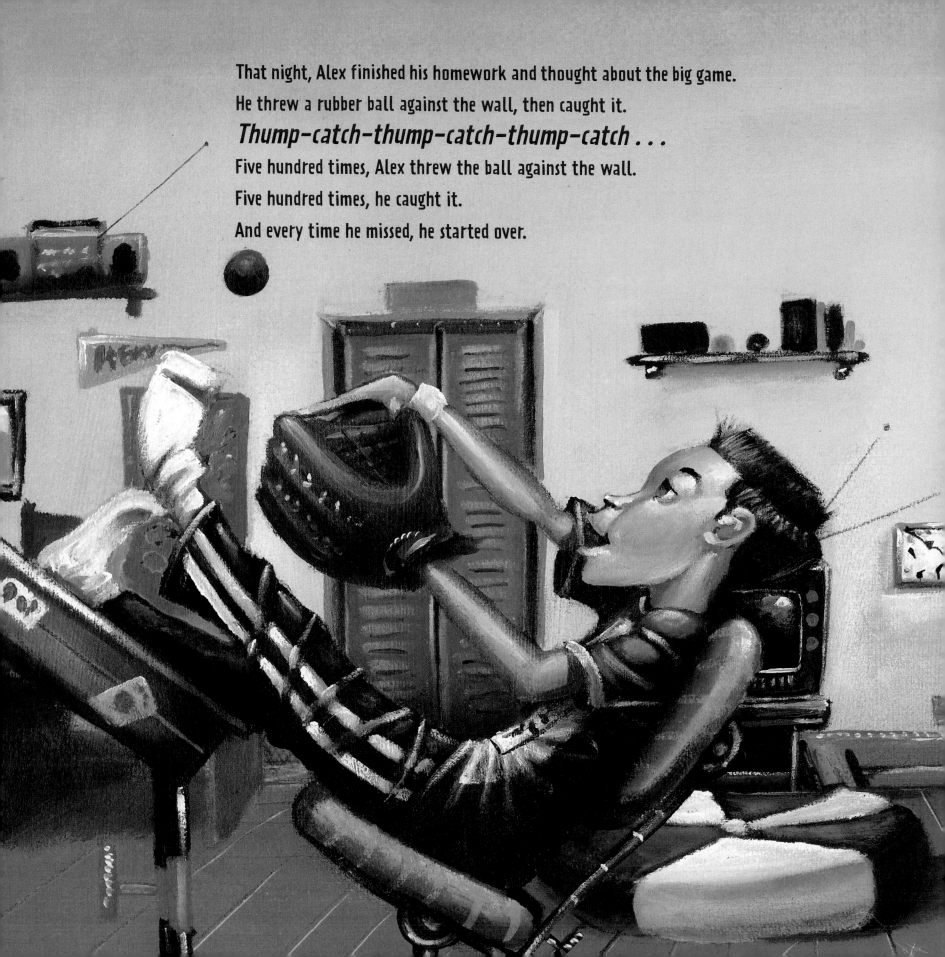

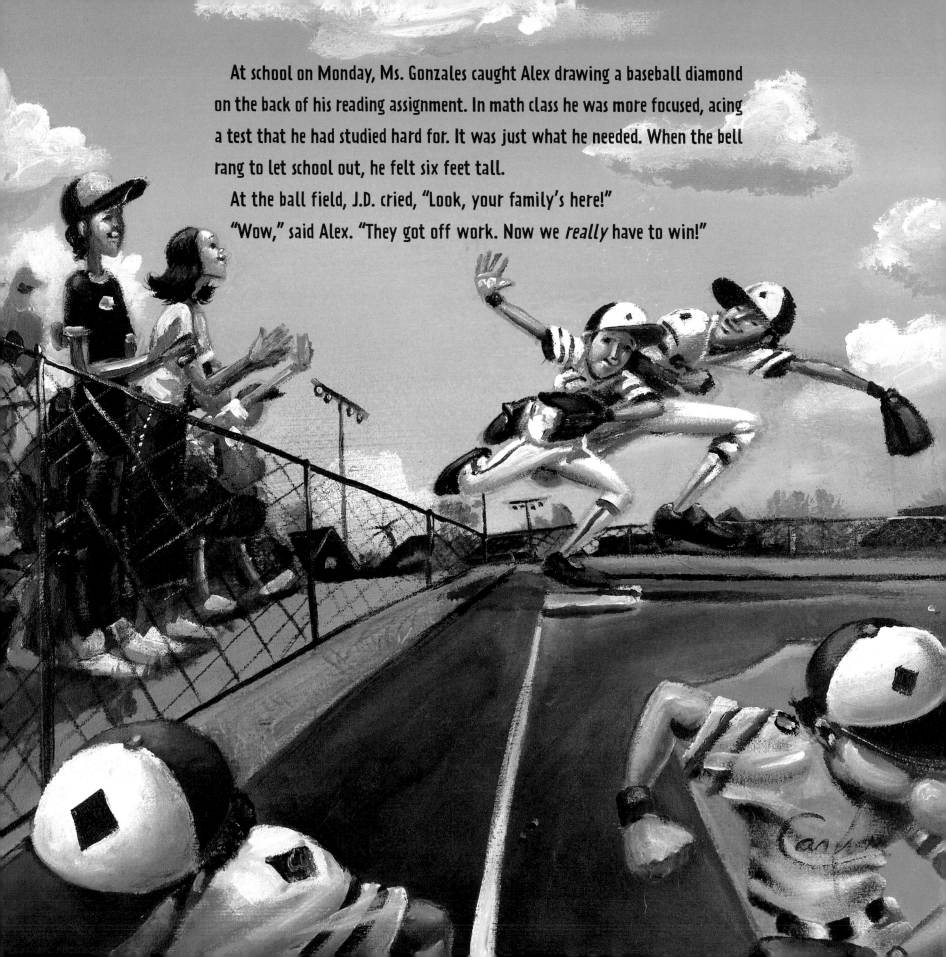

At school on Monday, Ms. Gonzales caught Alex drawing a baseball diamond on the back of his reading assignment. In math class he was more focused, acing a test that he had studied hard for. It was just what he needed. When the bell rang to let school out, he felt six feet tall.

At the ball field, J.D. cried, "Look, your family's here!"

"Wow," said Alex. "They got off work. Now we *really* have to win!"

But the Caribes trailed from the start. They were still down by two in the fourth when Alex lost a fly ball in the sun and missed it. The Stingrays scored another run. It was 4–1, and Alex's heart was pounding.

In the bottom of the last inning, Alex came up to bat. The Caribes were still down 4–1, but the bases were loaded. It was now or never. Alex swung at a pitch that was over his head.

"**Strike!**" called the umpire.

Alex watched the second pitch go by.

"**Strike!**" said the ump.

Alex swung at the third pitch. He swung strong

and level, with everything he had.

Crack! roared the bat.

Up, up, up the ball soared. Alex dropped his bat and ran, ran, ran.
As he approached second base, he heard . . .

Splash!

"Pool shot!" Joe yelled from the stands.

Alex's grand slam won the Caribes their very first championship.

"Yeeeaaaahhhhh!"

Alex yelled as he crossed home plate.

"We did it!"

He looked up into the stands and knew
that it didn't get any better than this.

Hi,

Thank you for reading Out of the Ballpark. It's a fictional story, but it's based on things I actually did—like getting up at 5 A.M. to practice my baseball fundamentals! I have always been a hard worker, both on and off the field. That's a big part of how I got to the Major Leagues. I also studied hard, stayed away from drugs, and showed respect for my friends and elders. That's my recipe for success, but you can use it, too. No matter what your dreams and goals, you can never go wrong if you give them all you've got.

Work hard,
Alex Rodriguez

Playing for Westminster Christian High School in Miami, where I also was on the football and basketball teams

Full of mischief at the beach

With my buddies from the All-Star team representing Miami in 1987. I'm second from left.

Wasn't I a cute baby?

When I was four, all I wanted for Christmas were my two front teeth!

Watch out, school, here I come!

A precious moment with my mom and dad

We had seven All-Stars on the Caribes when I was ten. I'm on the right.

J. D. Arteaga has been one of my closest friends for many years. That's J.D. in this story!

It was very exciting to be named National High School Player of the Year in 1993! Here I am with my brother, Joe; my mom; and my sister, Susy.

Mom gives me moral support before my first school dance, in junior high.

As a junior in high school, I got to play for the USA junior national team in Mexico!

Happy birthday, Mom! Here I am with my sister, Susy; Mom; and my brother, Joe.

ACKNOWLEDGMENTS

To my best friend and beautiful wife, Cynthia. Thank you for your support. It means the world to me. I'd like to thank my family, who sacrificed so much to allow me to chase my dreams—my mom, Lourdes; my sister, Susy; and my brother, Joe; Rich Hofman, for your guidance and mentorship; Lou Piniella, for teaching me to play the game the right way; all my coaches and the teammates I have played with since the first day I stepped foot on a baseball field; all my friends who have encouraged me and always been there for me, especially J. D., Pepi, and Gui; Scott Boras, my attorney, for your guidance and counsel; Steve Fortunato, my marketing agent, for bringing this book to life; the great team at HarperCollins Children's Books for putting it all together: Kate Jackson, Barbara Lalicki, Stephanie Bart-Horvath, Suzanne Daghlian, Audra Boltion, Ruiko Tokunaga, Mark Rifkin, Martha Rago, Maria Gomez, Dorothy Pietrewicz, and especially Rosemary Brosnan, my editor; Miriam Fabiancic; Frank Morrison, for taking me back to my childhood in Miami with your amazing illustrations; and finally, to all my fans around the world—my heartfelt thanks for supporting me all these years. —A.R.

My wife, Cynthia, daughter, Natasha, and me
at Family Day at Yankee Stadium, 2006

OUT OF THE BALLPARK

A portion of the author's and publisher's proceeds from this book will be donated to the AROD Family Foundation.